An AudioCraft Publishing, Inc. book

Book storage and warehouses provided by Chillermania!©
Indian River, Michigan

No part of this published work may be reproduced in whole or in part, by any means, without written permission from the publisher. For information regarding permission, contact: AudioCraft Publishing, Inc., PO Box 281, Topinabee Island, MI 49791

Freddie Fernortner, Fearless First Grader
Book 12: Frankenfreddie
ISBN 13-digit: 978-1-893699-64-9

Cover and illustrations by Cartoon Studios, Battle Creek, MI
Text and illustrations copyright 2013 by AudioCraft Publishing, Inc

Librarians/Media Specialists:
PCIP/MARC records available **free of charge** at
www.americanchillers.com

Cover illustration by Dwayne Harris
Cover layout and design by Sue Harring

Printed in USA

FRANKENFREDDIE

VISIT CHILLERMANIA!

WORLD HEADQUARTERS FOR BOOKS BY JOHNATHAN RAND!

Visit the HOME for books by Johnathan Rand! Featuring books, hats, shirts, bookmarks and other cool stuff not available anywhere else in the world! Plus, watch the American Chillers website for news of special events and signings at **CHILLERMANIA!** with author Johnathan Rand! Located in northern lower Michigan, on I-75! Take exit 313 . . . then south 1 mile! For more info, call (231) 238-0338. And be afraid! Be veeeery afraaaaaaiiiid . . . .

1

Halloween costumes can be funny. They can be silly and strange. Other Halloween costumes can be weird. Still, many costumes can be very, very cool.

But this isn't a story about one of those costumes. This is a story about Freddie Fernortner, fearless first grader, and a very terrifying Halloween costume. There is no doubt this story will scare many readers, so if you are easily frightened, you probably shouldn't read it. And even if you are very brave, don't ever read this story at night, as it might cause some very scary dreams.

But if you *are* brave and not easily frightened, continue reading. Brave readers will find this to be a story with many thrills, scary surprises, and much excitement.

One day, Freddie and his friends, Chipper, Darla, and Mr. Chewy, were walking to a nearby park. Mr. Chewy, Freddie's cat, followed closely behind the three first graders, chewing his gum and blowing bubbles. Most cats don't like gum, but not Mr. Chewy. He loves chewing gum and blowing bubbles. In fact, that's how he got his name.

"It's a beautiful day," Darla said as she gazed up into the blue sky. The sun was shining, and there wasn't a cloud in sight.

"It will be a great day to play in the park," Chipper said. "Maybe we'll meet some more of our friends."

"I hope so," said Freddie. "If we meet up with a few more of our friends, we might be able to play a game of basketball."

The three first graders and Mr. Chewy continued walking along the sidewalk. Suddenly, Freddie noticed something up ahead.

"Hey, guys," he said, pointing. "Take a look at that."

At the end of the block, a new sign had been placed in front of a building . . . a building that had been empty for a long, long time.

"It looks like a new store is coming to that old building," Chipper said.

"What does the sign say?" Darla asked.

"I can't read it," said Freddie. "It's too far away."

They continued to walk closer and closer to the building.

Closer and closer to the sign.

Closer and closer to something they never saw hiding in the bushes, waiting for them . . . .

2

The three first graders kept walking toward the new sign, trying to read it. Mr. Chewy scampered behind them, chewing his gum.

They stopped near a row of thick, dark green bushes that grew along the sidewalk. They had no idea hidden eyes were spying from inside the bushes.

Freddie stared at the sign in the distance, and spoke.

"I think it reads something about a costume shop," he said.

"A costume shop?" Darla asked. "Like, Halloween costumes?"

"Probably all kinds of costumes," Chipper said.

All the while, the unseen eyes in the bushes watched and waited.

"A costume shop would be cool!" Freddie said excitedly. "They might even have a Frankenstein costume! I can be Frankenfreddie for Halloween!"

"What should I be?" Darla wondered aloud. "A fairy princess?"

"If you want," Chipper said. "You could be a fairy princess, and I could be a pirate! Or a zombie!"

"Maybe I could be a zombie princess!" Darla said. "That would be funny and scary!"

"I'll bet they have all kinds of different costumes," Freddie said. "You can be anything you want for Halloween."

"But Freddie," Darla said. "It's not Halloween, yet."

"That's why we should start looking for good costumes right now," Freddie replied. "We need to find the perfect costumes before all of the good ones are taken."

All the while, as the three children chattered about Halloween, spooky nights, and scary costumes, they had no idea something was hiding in the bushes, waiting for just the right moment to leap out.

"Come on, guys," Freddie said. "Let's see what kind of costumes they have!"

The three first graders, followed by Mr. Chewy, began walking again . . . and it was at that very moment that the creature in the bushes made its move. It sprang from its hiding place so quickly that Freddie, Chipper, and Darla didn't even have time to scream for help.

3

Without any warning at all, Freddie was knocked to the ground. Darla shrieked, and even Chipper cried out.

Freddie landed on his side and quickly rolled to face his attacker.

"Salty!" he said, with relief, as he stared at the big, white, happy dog that stood over him. Salty belonged to a man who lived on Oak Street. He was a very friendly dog, and he liked Freddie very much. One time, when Freddie had a dog walking service, the man had hired Freddie, Chipper, and Darla to give Salty a bath, because he'd been digging in the garden and was very, very dirty.

"Holy cow," Chipper said. "Salty! You really scared us!"

The big, white dog began licking Freddie's face.

"Hey," Freddie laughed. "Knock it off, Salty!"

Freddie rolled to the side, then stood. Salty sat, wagging his tail and looking up at Freddie. Freddie patted the dog's head and scratched his ears.

Mr. Chewy, too, had been frightened. He had run to a nearby tree and climbed to a low branch, where he chewed his gum and watched with big, wide eyes.

"You shouldn't be running around without a leash," Freddie said to the dog. "You must've dug a hole under the fence again. Come on, buddy. I'll take you home."

"But Freddie," Darla said, "I thought we were going to the costume shop."

"We will," Freddie replied. "But we need to make sure that Salty gets home safe."

"Why don't you take Salty home," Chipper said, "and Darla and I will go to the costume shop. We'll take Mr. Chewy with us and meet you there after you take Salty home."

That was fine with Freddie. He and Salty were good pals, and he didn't mind taking him back to his owner on Oak Street.

Chipper and Darla watched as Freddie and the big, white dog walked away, side-by-side, on the sidewalk.

"I had no idea Salty was in the bushes,"

Darla said. "He really freaked me out."

"Me, too," Chipper said. "I'm glad it wasn't a mountain lion or a grizzly bear. He would've had us for lunch."

Now that the dog was gone, Mr. Chewy climbed down from the tree and joined Chipper and Darla. The three walked to the costume shop and stopped in front of it, staring at the new sign.

"Merlin's Magical Costume Shop," Chipper read aloud.

"Opening soon," Darla read.

"Rats," said Chipper. "It's not open yet. I really wanted to see some costumes."

"Let's look through the windows," Darla said. "We might be able to see something."

The two first graders approached the store. Mr. Chewy stayed on the sidewalk, chewing his gum and blowing bubbles.

They walked up to a dark window.

They leaned toward the glass.

They peered inside.

Suddenly, the front door of the store opened wide, and standing in the doorway was a horrible, hairy monster!

4

Darla shrieked. Chipper leapt back. Both children turned and started to run, but were stopped suddenly by a man's voice.

"Wait!" a man shouted. "I didn't mean to scare you!"

Chipper and Darla turned around to see the giant, hairy monster reach up . . . and pull off his head!

Except, of course, it wasn't his

head . . . it was only a mask! When the man removed it from his head, he didn't look so scary anymore. It was only the face of an old man, with white hair, a white beard, and a white mustache. His blue eyes twinkled, and he smiled warmly.

"I'm sorry," the old man said. "I'm Merlin, and this is my store. I saw you peeking through the window, and I wanted to say 'hello' to you. I've been trying on a few of my masks, and I forgot I was wearing one."

"You really freaked us out," Darla said. "We thought you were a real monster."

Merlin shook his head. "It's just a mask," he said. "And a good one, too, eh? I make all of my costumes and masks myself."

"Wow," Chipper said.

Behind them, Freddie had returned from taking Salty home. He was walking up the sidewalk toward them. Mr. Chewy remained sitting on the sidewalk, chewing his gum.

"What's going on?" Freddie asked as he stopped next to Chipper and Darla.

"I frightened your friends," Merlin said. "Of course, I didn't mean to, and I'm very sorry."

"That's a really cool monster mask," Freddie said.

"He makes all of his own costumes and masks," Darla said.

Merlin put the mask back on and raised his arms in the air. He really *did* look terrifying. But now that the three first graders knew it was only a mask, it didn't scare them.

"Wow!" said Freddie. "You really look like a scary monster! What other costumes and masks do you have?"

Merlin shook his head. "None for you,

I'm afraid," he said. "All of my costumes and masks are for adults."

The three first graders were very disappointed. They'd hoped to find some fun Halloween costumes.

Seeing their sadness, Merlin smiled. He hated to see unhappy children.

"I'll tell you what I'll do," Merlin said. "Why don't I see if I can put together something. Maybe I can make a simple costume for each of you."

"Like a Frankenstein monster costume?" Freddie asked. His eyes were wide and shiny.

The man stroked his white beard. "Maybe," he said. "I will do my best. Come back next week, when my store is officially open."

All week long, Freddie was so excited that he couldn't think of anything else. He couldn't wait until the costume shop opened and he could go inside. He dreamed of having the perfect costume for Halloween.

Little did he know that his perfect Halloween costume would turn into something else: the perfect nightmare!

5

Finally, the big day arrived. It was the grand opening of *Merlin's Magical Costume Shop*. Freddie, Chipper, Darla, and Mr. Chewy gathered on the Fernortner's porch.

"I've been waiting all week for this day!" Chipper said.

"Me, too!" said Darla.

"I can't wait!" Freddie said. "Let's go!"

The day was sunny and bright, and the

three first graders chattered like chipmunks as they walked along the sidewalk. Mr. Chewy followed close behind, chewing gum and blowing bubbles.

"I wonder if Merlin was able to make me a Frankenstein monster costume," Freddie said.

"I wonder what he made for me," chimed Chipper.

"And me, too," said Darla.

"Wait a minute," Freddie said. He stopped walking, and Chipper and Darla stopped, too. Mr. Chewy also stopped and sat on the sidewalk.

"What's wrong?" asked Chipper.

Freddie pointed at his cat. "Mr. Chewy won't have a costume," Freddie said.

"Whoever heard of a cat wearing a costume?" Darla replied.

"Would you like to wear a costume, Mr. Chewy?" Freddie asked.

Mr. Chewy shook his head and blew a bubble. The bubble popped, and the cat continued chewing his gum.

"That settles that," Freddie said. "No costume for Mr. Chewy."

The three began walking again, and Mr. Chewy followed. Soon, they were standing in front of the new costume shop. In the window was a lighted sign that read: OPEN.

"Let's go!" Freddie said, and the three first graders charged to the front door and burst into the store.

They stopped.

Mr. Chewy scampered in. He stopped at Freddie's feet.

"Oh, my goodness," Darla whispered, and the three first graders looked around.

There were costumes and masks everywhere. They were on shelves, hanging from walls, and even hanging from the ceiling. Ghosts, alien creatures, clowns, mummies, superheroes . . . every type of costume you could think of. The three first graders could only stare in wonder and amazement.

Finally, Darla spoke.

"Where is Merlin?" she asked. "I don't see him around."

They looked around the store, but they saw no sign of the curious, white-haired man they had met the week before.

"He's got to be around here somewhere," said Chipper. "I don't think he would leave his store with the door unlocked and the 'open' sign on."

Darla stepped around a rack of clothing and slowly made her way toward a long counter with a cash register.

"I have a funny feeling about this," she said as she looked around. "Merlin has to be around here somewhere, but I don't see him."

"Merlin?" Chipper called out as he looked around the store. "Are you around?"

Darla peered around the counter and suddenly drew in a thick, deep breath.

"Oh, no!" she cried. *"Freddie! Chipper! The store owner is here! He's behind the counter! I think he's dead!"*

6

Freddie raced to Darla's side, followed by Chipper and Mr. Chewy. The three first graders and the cat stared at the body of Merlin, laying on a long couch behind the counter.

"He's not moving," Darla whispered. *"He must be dead."*

They continued staring at Merlin. He didn't move.

Then, Mr. Chewy made a sudden leap, landing on the old man's chest. With his paw, he began playing with the man's long, white beard.

"Mr. Chewy, no," Freddie whispered. He was just about to pick up his cat when suddenly, Merlin's eyes flew open. When he saw Mr. Chewy, the old man shrieked so loudly that he not only scared the three first graders, but Mr. Chewy, too! The cat leapt into the air, and Freddie scooped up Mr. Chewy in his arms.

"Goodness!" the old man exclaimed. "Children! Where did you come from?"

"Our houses," Darla replied.

The old man sat up and looked around. He seemed confused until he realized where he was.

"Ah," he said. "I fell asleep. I sat down

to rest, but I must have been more tired than I thought."

"Your store sign says you're open," Chipper said.

"Indeed, indeed," the old man said as he stood. "Today is my grand opening. What can I help you children with?"

"Last week," Freddie said, "you told us that you'd try to make some costumes for us. I was hoping you made me a Frankenstein monster costume. I want to be Frankenfreddie for Halloween."

Merlin's eyes lit up. "Ah, yes!" he said. "And I've created the most wonderful costumes for each of you!"

"Really?" Darla said, clasping her hands together.

Merlin nodded. "Yes. And I think you're going to like what I've come up with."

Merlin walked to a desk with several drawers that was against the back wall. He opened one of the drawers and reached inside.

"For you, my young friend," Merlin said, nodding toward Chipper, "I have put together items for you to be a mad scientist."

"Super cool!" Chipper said as the old man handed Chipper a small box. Inside was a crazy, orange-colored wig and a pair of safety goggles.

"And for you, young lady," he said to Darla, "I have the perfect wig and dress. You will be the bride of Frankenstein!"

Merlin removed a large wig with brown and white hair from the drawer, along with a faded white dress that was ripped in several places.

"Wow!" Darla said.

Merlin handed the wig and the dress to

Darla.

"And for you," Merlin said, smiling at Freddie, "I have just what you wanted. You will be the Frankenstein monster for Halloween!"

Merlin reached into the drawer and pulled out a small box. It contained a few bandages, a couple of fake scars with stitches, and two curious bolts.

"These bolts," Merlin said, "are made out of foam. They've been painted silver, so they look real."

He plucked a bolt from the box and held it up for the children to see.

"Wow," Freddie breathed.

"They are very light," Merlin explained. "And here," Merlin continued as he picked up a small plastic bottle, "is some glue to use so the bolts stick to your neck. But don't worry:

it's safe. Normally, you wouldn't want to put glue on your skin. But this is a special glue. Plain old water will make the bolts come off easily."

Freddie was breathless.

"I'm going to be Frankenfreddie!" he said loudly. "Can we try on our costumes?"

"Certainly!" Merlin beamed. "I think the three of you are going to look terrific!"

But it was not to be.

Oh, Chipper was going to look terrific, all right.

And Darla was going to look terrific.

But Freddie Fernortner, fearless first grader, was *not* going to look terrific. He was going to look horrifying. He didn't know it yet, but in just a few moments, his awful nightmare was about to begin.

7

Here's what happened:

Merlin excused himself to retrieve an item from a back room, leaving the three first graders in the store. They began chatting excitedly among themselves, while Mr. Chewy looked on.

Darla slipped the tattered dress over her clothing. Then, she put on her wig and looked at herself in a nearby mirror.

"You look great!" Chipper said. "Help me with my mad scientist wig."

Darla helped Chipper with his orange wig, and then he put on his safety goggles. With his wild, orange hair and his safety goggles in place, he really did look like a mad scientist.

Freddie attached the fake scars to his forehead. Then, he put bandages over a few of them. After dabbing a bit of glue to each bolt, he placed one on each side of his neck. They easily stuck to his skin.

"What do you think?" he asked his friends.

"Freddie!" Darla replied. "You look scary!"

"Do I look like Frankenfreddie?" Freddie asked.

"You sure do!" Chipper and Darla said.

But Freddie began to feel funny. He felt a strange tingling sensation all through his body, from the top of his head to the tips of his toes.

"I'm feeling kind of weird," he said to Chipper and Darla.

"You look strange," Darla said.

"Yeah," said Chipper. "Your skin looks like it's changing color."

Freddie turned to look at himself in the mirror . . . and that's when something frightening happened.

Freddie started to grow.

Darla gasped.

Chipper gasped.

Mr. Chewy stopped chewing his gum.

Freddie grew taller.

And taller.

Taller still.

And as his body got bigger, so did his clothing and shoes! Soon, he was more than twice his height, and he turned to look down at his friends.

He flashed a terrible grin.

Then, without a word, he turned, raised his arms straight out, and stumbled toward the front door.

Chipper and Darla were horrified. Mr. Chewy leapt into Darla's arms.

"Holy cow!" Chipper blurted.

"Merlin!" Darla shouted. "Merlin! Help! Something is really, really wrong!"

But there was no reply. Darla, Chipper, and Mr. Chewy could only watch as Frankenfreddie pushed open the front door and went outside.

Things were about to get very, very bad.

And very, very scary.

8

Chipper and Darla raced to the store window, followed by Mr. Chewy. The two first graders and the cat peered outside. Frankenfreddie was slowly stumbling along the sidewalk, his arms outstretched.

"I must be dreaming!" Darla said.

Chipper shook his head. "This is no dream," he said. "This is a nightmare."

"How did Freddie get so big?" Darla

asked.

"I don't know," Chipper replied. "But it happened right after he put those bolts on his neck."

Darla pressed her nose against the window. Chipper turned his head.

"Merlin!" he shouted. "We need help! Something is really, really wrong!"

"Something awful has happened!" shouted Darla.

But there was no sign of the old store owner. Their shouts were answered only by silence.

"He really did it," Chipper said softly as he watched Freddie stumble along.

"Did what?" asked Darla.

"He wanted to be Frankenfreddie for Halloween," answered Chipper. "It looks like he got his wish."

Outside, Freddie continued his monster walk along the sidewalk. A bird flew over his head. When Frankenfreddie saw this, he stopped. Then, he angrily threw his arms into the air as if he were reaching for the bird. He let out a loud growl that caused Chipper and Darla to shudder. Even Mr. Chewy flinched.

Then, the two first graders saw something else: a woman, talking on her phone while she was walking her little, white dog. She was at the end of the block, and she was heading toward Freddie.

Frankenfreddie began moving again. He'd spotted the woman and her dog and was headed in their direction.

"Oh, no!" Darla said. "She's talking on her phone and not paying attention! She doesn't see Freddie!"

Chipper raced to the door and threw it

open. Darla followed. But just as Chipper was about to shout a warning, the unthinkable happened.

Freddie . . . who had now turned into a real Frankenstein monster . . . charged the woman. By the time the woman saw the giant, scary Frankenfreddie heading toward her, Chipper and Darla knew it was going to be too late to warn her. The poor woman and her dog were about to become Freddie's first victims.

9

The woman shrieked and dropped her phone. Her little, white dog yelped.

Freddie lunged, and just in the nick of time, the woman and the dog darted to the side, barely escaping the clutches of the horrifying monster. She quickly snapped up her phone from the grass and fled with her little, white dog. They ran away as fast as they could.

Meanwhile, Frankenfreddie had stopped on the sidewalk. His arms were stretched out in front of him. He turned, looking a little confused. He seemed surprised that the woman and her dog had gotten away.

"We've got to do something!" Chipper said.

"I'll go find Merlin!" Darla said.

"I'll stay here and see what Freddie does!" said Chipper.

Darla spun and raced through the costume shop. She stopped at an open door leading to the back room.

"Merlin?" Darla called out. "Merlin? Are you here?"

Darla stepped into the room. It was filled with all sorts of boxes, costumes, and masks. There were several chairs and a desk at the far wall and another door that was closed.

Again, Darla called out. "Merlin? Are you around? Something's wrong with Freddie! Merlin?"

Still, there was no answer. It was as if Merlin had vanished into thin air.

Quickly, Darla raced back through the costume shop to the front door. It was open, and Chipper was standing in the doorway. Mr. Chewy stood in the doorway, too.

"I can't find Merlin!" Darla said.

Down the street, Freddie had turned around and was walking back toward the costume shop.

"What are we going to do?" Darla asked. Her voice trembled. She sounded very frightened.

"We're just a couple of kids," Chipper said. "I don't think there's anything we *can* do. Maybe we should call the police."

"We can't call the police on Freddie!" Darla said. "He hasn't done anything wrong!"

"I know," Chipper said. "But we've got to find a way to stop him before someone gets hurt."

While they watched, terrified, Frankenfreddie kept walking up the sidewalk.

A car approached.

It slowed.

Seated in the driver's side was a man. He was looking out the window at Freddie. The man's eyes were wide, and his mouth hung open. He couldn't believe what he was seeing.

Then, he stopped the car.

Frankenfreddie stopped. He spotted the man in the car.

The man stared at Frankenfreddie.

Frankenfreddie stared at the man.

Without warning, Frankenfreddie

stumbled into the street, stopping in front of the man's car. He threw his arms into the air and let out a loud, shrieking growl. Darla and Chipper had never heard their friend make such an awful, horrifying sound.

But what happened next was absolutely terrifying.

10

The man in the car was frozen in terror. He sat in the driver's seat, his hands on the steering wheel, staring at the horrifying monster in front of his car.

Slowly, Frankenfreddie raised his right foot and placed it on the front bumper of the car. Then, he carefully stepped up, placing his left foot on the car hood! He raised his right foot. Frankenfreddie was now standing on the hood of the man's car!

"Oh, no!" Chipper said.

"This is horrible!" said Darla. "This is just horrible!"

The two first graders could only watch as Freddie let out another piercing growl that echoed through the neighborhood.

Terrified, the man behind the wheel threw open the car door. He leapt out and ran into a nearby yard. Then, he turned and stopped.

Frankenfreddie walked over the hood, up the windshield, over the top of the car, and to the trunk. He stopped on the trunk and began bouncing around, almost as if he was dancing. Chipper and Darla didn't know whether to scream in terror or laugh out loud.

Then, Frankenfreddie leapt off the trunk and landed on the street. He paused for a moment before stumbling to the curb and back onto the sidewalk.

Meanwhile, the man who had fled from his car watched warily. As the monster began to move away, he took a cautious step forward. Suddenly, he started running until he reached his car, where he leapt inside, slammed the door, and roared away.

"Whew," Chipper said. "That was a close call. I thought that man was in big trouble."

"Chipper," Darla said, "we've got to do something. Pretty soon, someone is going to get hurt. Or Freddie will hurt himself."

"Or us," said Chipper.

The two children watched as Frankenfreddie began stumbling up the sidewalk. His arms were outstretched, and he was mumbling and moaning.

"Chipper," Darla said, "what if Freddie stays like that forever?"

It was a chilling thought.

"I'll bet those bolts on his neck have something to do with it," Chipper said. "If only we could find a way to take those bolts off, I bet he would be normal again."

"I'm afraid to get close to him," Darla said.

"There's got to be a way," Chipper said.

While they watched Frankenfreddie stumble along the sidewalk, both first graders were deep in thought.

Then, Chipper saw something that gave him an idea.

"I think I've got it!" Chipper said.

"You do?" replied Darla.

"Yes!" said Chipper.

Chipper's plan was a good one, but it

was dangerous, and both first graders agreed that it might not work.

But they had no choice. They couldn't find Merlin, and they simply *had* to rescue their friend and try to make him normal again.

Was Chipper's plan going to work?

He and Darla were about to find out.

11

This was Chipper's plan:

A couple of blocks away, a large tree grew in the middle of a big yard. Chipper would get the attention of Frankenfreddie and try to get him to follow. Meanwhile, Darla would race to the tree and hide behind the trunk. When she was in place and ready, Chipper would lead Freddie into the yard and pass by the tree. At the right moment, Darla would put out her leg and trip Freddie, causing him to fall to the grass. Then, Chipper would pounce and quickly pluck the bolts from Freddie's neck.

"But Chipper," Darla said, "what if Freddie doesn't come after you?"

"I think he will," Chipper said. "Did you see how he went after that woman with the dog? And the man in the car? So, I'm pretty sure he'll chase after me. He'll follow me into the yard, and I'll lead him by the tree. You'll trip him, he'll fall, and I'll yank the bolts from his neck."

"If you say so," Darla said. "I hope it works. I hope he changes back to his normal self."

"You stay here until I can get Freddie's attention," said Chipper. "When he starts to follow me, run over and hide behind that tree."

Chipper darted out the door. Soon, he was racing down the sidewalk.

"Hey, Freddie!" he shouted as he ran. "Frankenfreddie!"

Hearing his name, Frankenfreddie stopped. He paused, looking around curiously.

"Freddie!" Chipper called again, still running toward the giant monster.

Frankenfreddie turned.

He saw Chipper.

Chipper stopped.

Then, just as Chipper had hoped, Frankenfreddie began stumbling in his direction.

When Darla saw this, she sprang into action. She and Mr. Chewy bounded across several front yards and ran to the tree. There, she hid behind the trunk. Mr. Chewy climbed to a low branch and sat.

Frankenfreddie moved slowly, dragging his feet and stumbling along the sidewalk. Chipper stayed in front of him, leading him along. Several times, Chipper glanced across the street to make sure Darla was ready. He saw her peering around the trunk, and he saw Mr. Chewy sitting on a low branch.

All the while, the giant-sized Frankenfreddie followed after Chipper. His arms were stretched out, and his movements were jerky.

Soon, they were close to the tree.

"Are you ready, Darla?" Chipper called out. He couldn't see her because she was hiding behind the tree trunk.

"Yep!" Darla shouted back.

Chipper ran through the grass, keeping a safe distance in front of Frankenfreddie.

When Chipper passed the tree, he saw Darla hiding behind the trunk.

"He's right behind me," Chipper whispered to Darla, and he continued walking.

"I know," Darla whispered back.

Then, Freddie passed by the tree. As he did, Darla stuck out her foot, catching Freddie's ankle.

Freddie stumbled.

Then, he fell forward, falling into the grass face-first!

Chipper didn't waste any time. He turned around, raced to Freddie, and leapt onto his back.

"Hurry, Chipper, hurry!" Darla said. "Take the bolts off!"

But it was too late. Freddie had already risen to his knees, with Chipper's arms wrapped around his neck.

Freddie stood, lifting Chipper completely off the ground!

"The bolts won't come off!" Chipper shouted as he struggled to work them free. "I can't get them off his neck!"

It was horrible. All Chipper could do was hang onto Freddie's neck and prepare himself for the wildest ride of his life!

12

Darla leapt out from behind the tree.

"Chipper, let go!" she cried.

"I can't!" Chipper shouted. "This might be our only chance to save Freddie!"

Frankenfreddie was stumbling wildly all over the yard, flailing his arms about. He was trying to grasp Chipper, who held firmly to Frankenfreddie's neck.

Then, it happened. Chipper was able to

grasp each of the bolts in his hands. He pulled and pulled . . . and they came off!

Instantly, Chipper fell from Frankenfreddie's back, where he landed in the grass. He stared in disbelief at the two bolts in his hands.

But what happened next was the most shocking part.

Frankenfreddie was no longer stumbling around. He had stopped, and he was staring at Chipper with a curious look in his eyes.

Then, Freddie began to shrink. Smaller and smaller, smaller still, until he was his normal size once again. Then, he sat down in the grass.

Darla peered out from behind the tree.

Mr. Chewy still sat on the branch, watching Freddie, slowly waving his tail back and forth. Then, the cat scampered down the trunk and cautiously approached Freddie.

"Freddie?" Chipper asked. "Are you all right?"

Freddie paused and looked around. Then, he spoke.

"How did I get outside?" he asked.

"You walked here," Chipper said.

"But I was in the store only a moment ago," Freddie said. "Now I'm outside in the grass."

Darla stepped out from behind the tree. "You don't remember how you got out here?" she asked.

Freddie shook his head. "No," he replied. "The last thing I remember, I was in the costume shop. I was putting those bolts on my neck, and now I'm out here."

Chipper gasped. "You don't remember anything that just happened?" he asked.

Again, Freddie shook his head. "No," he answered.

"When you put those bolts on your neck," Chipper said, "you grew super tall. You turned into a real Frankenstein monster!"

Freddie's jaw dropped. "I did?" he asked.

Chipper and Darla nodded. Even Mr. Chewy bobbed his head as he sat on the tree limb.

"You even scared a woman and her dog," Darla said. "And a man in a car."

"I don't remember that at all," Freddie said, scratching his head. "The last thing I remember, I was putting the bolts on my neck."

"You turned into Frankenfreddie," Darla said. "Chipper changed you back when he pulled the bolts off."

"I wonder how it happened," Freddie said.

In moments, he would have his answer.

13

Just as Darla was about to speak, they heard a shout. Freddie, Chipper, Darla, and Mr. Chewy turned to see Merlin standing in the doorway of his store, holding the door open. He was smiling.

"Are you having fun?" he called out.

"Um, sort of," Darla replied. "Where did you go?"

"Just out back," Merlin replied. "I have

another storage unit filled with more costumes behind the store. Why? Is something wrong?"

Freddie got to his feet, and the three first graders and Mr. Chewy walked to the store and stopped in front.

"Freddie turned into a monster when he put those bolts on his neck," Chipper said.

"And he scared a woman with a dog and a man in a car," said Darla. "We were scared, too."

"Good heavens!" Merlin said. "I must've given you the wrong bolts!"

"What do you mean?" Freddie replied.

"Do you still have the bolts?" asked Merlin.

Chipper nodded and held out his hand. Both bolts sat in his palm.

"Just as I suspected," Merlin said as he plucked the two bolts from Chipper's hand.

"What?" Darla asked.

"These are the bolts from the *real* Frankenstein monster," he said. "I bought them from a collector years ago. I knew I had them somewhere. They must've gotten mixed up with the other pair. Very dangerous. They are said to have strange, magical powers."

"Yeah," Chipper said. "They made Freddie grow huge!"

Darla nodded. "It was scary," she said.

"I think I know how to fix this," Merlin said. "Come inside."

Freddie, Darla, Chipper, and Mr. Chewy followed Merlin into the store. They made their way to the back where the large desk sat. Once again, Merlin opened one of the drawers and began looking through it.

"Nope, nope," he said. "That's not it. That's not it, either. Ah! Here it is!"

Merlin pulled out a small box and opened it.

"Here we are!" he said, showing the box to the three first graders.

Inside the box were two bolts.

"These are the bolts I meant to give you," Merlin said. "These are costume bolts. Here, Freddie," he said, holding out the box. "These are yours to keep. And don't worry: nothing bad will happen with these."

Freddie took the box and plucked out one of the bolts. It was silver colored and very light.

"Are you sure?" he asked.

"Absolutely," Merlin said. "And you all three may keep your costumes so you can wear them for Halloween."

"Cool!" Chipper said.

"Yeah, thanks, Merlin," said Darla.

Freddie removed the fake stitches and bandages from his head. Darla slipped out of her bride of Frankenstein dress and took off her wig. Chipper removed his goggles and his orange wig.

"Thanks for the great costumes, Merlin," Freddie said.

Merlin waved. "You're very welcome," he said with a grin. "You three have a fun Halloween."

They said good-bye to their new friend and left the store, each carrying their costumes.

"This sure has been a crazy day," Chipper said.

"We were really scared, Freddie," Darla said.

"What are we going to do tomorrow?" asked Chipper.

"Something safe," said Darla.

"I've already got a great idea," Freddie said. "And there's no way we can get into any trouble."

"Tell us!" Darla said.

"Yeah, tell us!" said Chipper.

"My grandpa and grandma sent me a box of small, plastic dinosaurs," Freddie said. "We can play with them in my sandbox and pretend we've gone back in time!"

"That sounds like fun!" Darla said.

"Yeah, Freddie!" said Chipper. "And there's no way we'll get into trouble."

And the three first graders, followed by Mr. Chewy, walked home . . . not knowing that, the very next day, big trouble would find them once again. And once again, Freddie Fernortner and his pals were about to have another wild—and scary—adventure!

NEXT:

Freddie Fernortner

FEARLESS FIRST GRADER

BOOK 13:

DAY OF THE DINOSAURS

CONTINUE READING FOR A FREE PREVIEW!

1

The day was sunny and bright as Freddie Fernortner, fearless first grader, sat on his porch. Beside him, Freddie's cat, Mr. Chewy, also sat, chewing gum and blowing bubbles. Most cats don't like gum, but not Mr. Chewy. He loved bubblegum, and he chewed it all day long. That's how he got his name.

"It won't be long now," Freddie said to his cat. "Chipper and Darla should be here any minute."

In Freddie's hands was a cardboard box. Inside of the box were five small, colorful, toy dinosaurs made of plastic. They had been given to him by his grandparents as a gift. Today, the three first graders planned to place them in Freddie's sandbox and pretend that they had traveled back in time, millions of years, back to the time of dinosaurs.

Freddie picked up one of the dinosaurs. It was a bright green Tyrannosaurus rex. Even though it was a toy and made of plastic, it looked very scary.

"Hey Freddie!" He heard a voice shout. Freddie looked up to see his two best friends, Chipper and Darla, racing toward him along the sidewalk.

Freddie put the dinosaur in the box, stood, and smiled.

"Are you ready to travel back in time?" he asked eagerly.

Chipper and Darla stopped when they reached Freddie's porch. Both first graders were panting and out of breath.

"I am!" Darla said.

"I am, too!" said Chipper.

Freddie raised the box. "I've got the dinosaurs, right here," he said. "Let's go!"

The three first graders, followed by Mr. Chewy, darted off the porch, around the side of the house, and into Freddie's backyard. Several large trees grew, providing shade on hot summer days. Near one of the trees was a swing set, and next to the swing set was Freddie's sandbox.

Freddie, Chipper, and Darla sat inside the sandbox. Freddie placed his box of plastic toy dinosaurs in the sand. The three first graders began taking the dinosaurs from the box and placing them in the sandbox.

"Look at this one," Chipper said as he held up a plastic dinosaur with wings. "It's a flying dinosaur." He waved it around a few times in the air, as if the dinosaur was actually flying. Then, he placed it in the sandbox.

A breeze rustled the leaves in the trees. Mr. Chewy jumped into the sandbox and sat down. He chewed his gum and blew bubbles, watching the three first graders place the dinosaurs around the sandbox.

Soon, there was only one dinosaur left in the box. Freddie picked it up.

"This is the last one," he said as he looked down at the plastic dinosaurs in the sand. He reached out to put the dinosaur in the sandbox, not knowing that something horrifying was about to happen.

Other books by Johnathan Rand:

Michigan Chillers:

#1: Mayhem on Mackinac Island
#2: Terror Stalks Traverse City
#3: Poltergeists of Petoskey
#4: Aliens Attack Alpena
#5: Gargoyles of Gaylord
#6: Strange Spirits of St. Ignace
#7: Kreepy Klowns of Kalamazoo
#8: Dinosaurs Destroy Detroit
#9: Sinister Spiders of Saginaw
#10: Mackinaw City Mummies
#11: Great Lakes Ghost Ship
#12: AuSable Alligators
#13: Gruesome Ghouls of Grand Rapids
#14: Bionic Bats of Bay City
#15: Calumet Copper Creatures
#16: Catastrophe in Caseville

American Chillers:

#1: The Michigan Mega-Monsters
#2: Ogres of Ohio
#3: Florida Fog Phantoms
#4: New York Ninjas
#5: Terrible Tractors of Texas
#6: Invisible Iguanas of Illinois
#7: Wisconsin Werewolves
#8: Minnesota Mall Mannequins
#9: Iron Insects Invade Indiana
#10: Missouri Madhouse
#11: Poisonous Pythons Paralyze Pennsylvania
#12: Dangerous Dolls of Delaware
#13: Virtual Vampires of Vermont
#14: Creepy Condors of California
#15: Nebraska Nightcrawlers
#16: Alien Androids Assault Arizona
#17: South Carolina Sea Creatures
#18: Washington Wax Museum
#19: North Dakota Night Dragons
#20: Mutant Mammoths of Montana
#21: Terrifying Toys of Tennessee
#22: Nuclear Jellyfish of New Jersey
#23: Wicked Velociraptors of West Virginia
#24: Haunting in New Hampshire
#25: Mississippi Megalodon
#26: Oklahoma Outbreak
#27: Kentucky Komodo Dragons
#28: Curse of the Connecticut Coyotes
#29: Oregon Oceanauts

American Chillers (cont'd)

#31: The Nevada Nightmare Novel
#32: Idaho Ice Beast
#33: Monster Mosquitoes of Maine
#34: Savage Dinosaurs of South Dakota
#35: Maniac Martians Marooned in Massachusetts
#36. Carnivorous Crickets of Colorado
#37: The Underground Undead of Utah
#38: The Wicked Waterpark of Wyoming

Freddie Fernortner, Fearless First Grader:

#1: The Fantastic Flying Bicycle
#2: The Super-Scary Night Thingy
#3: A Haunting We Will Go
#4: Freddie's Dog Walking Service
#5: The Big Box Fort
#6: Mr. Chewy's Big Adventure
#7: The Magical Wading Pool
#8: Chipper's Crazy Carnival
#9: Attack of the Dust Bunnies from Outer Space!
#10: The Pond Monster
#11: Tadpole Trouble
#12: Frankenfreddie

Adventure Club series:

#1: Ghost in the Graveyard
#2: Ghost in the Grand
#3: The Haunted Schoolhouse

For Teens:

PANDEMIA: A novel of the
bird flu and the end of the world
(written with Christopher Knight)

American Chillers Double Thrillers:

Vampire Nation &
Attack of the Monster Venus Melon

WATCH FOR MORE FREDDIE FERNORTNER, FEARLESS FIRST GRADER BOOKS, COMING SOON!